NANCY DREW

Movie MYSTERY

by Irene Kilpatrick
based on the screenplay by Tiffany Paulsen
and on the characters created by Carolyn Keene

Simon Spotlight
New York   London   Toronto   Sydney

Based on the movie NANCY DREW by Warner Bros. Entertainment Inc.

SIMON SPOTLIGHT
An imprint of Simon & Schuster Children's Publishing Division
1230 Avenue of the Americas, New York, New York 10020
NANCY DREW © Warner Bros. Entertainment Inc. NANCY DREW is a
trademark of Simon & Schuster, Inc. (s07)
Manufactured in the United States of America
First Edition
10 9 8 7 6 5 4 3 2 1
ISBN-13: 978-1-4169-3901-6
ISBN-10: 1-4169-3901-6

Sunday

Hello from Hollywood! I've just arrived with my dad at Draycott Mansion, where we'll be spending the next few months. On the way here Dad made me promise not to do any sleuthing—but he doesn't know that this mansion is the site of a *big* mystery! It was here that something happened to the famous movie star Dehlia Draycott twenty-five years ago. Can I really keep my promise?

Monday, 7:00 p.m.

Last night I was unpacking in my new room when I heard a strange patter. It sounded like footsteps! I went into the hall to investigate, but no one was there. When I returned to my room, my folder full of Dehlia Draycott clippings had disappeared!

Name: Dehlia Draycott

Occupation: Movie actress

Notes: Was loved by many, but never married.

The Mystery: At the height of her fame she disappeared for 5 months and then threw a giant party upon her return. But she never went downstairs to greet her guests. Later that night she was found floating in the pool.

Monday, 11:00 p.m.
CLUE: The Letter

A Dehlia Draycott Reading List:
* The Well of Loneliness
* The Light in the Darkness
* Embracing Solitude
* The Vincent Price Cookbook
* The Life and Death of Dehlia
  Draycott

I just heard the footsteps again! This time I thought they were coming from the attic, so I went upstairs. Just like last night I didn't see anyone. But I did find a sleuth's goldmine! Piled all around the attic was Dehlia memorabilia: boxes, books, and other things. When I picked up one of the books, a letter fell out:

> Z . . .
> I'm sorry to have vanished like I did. I know you have been looking for me. Something has happened last week. I can't be the Dehlia I was anymore. I'm writing a new will. I need to make provisions for someone else. —D

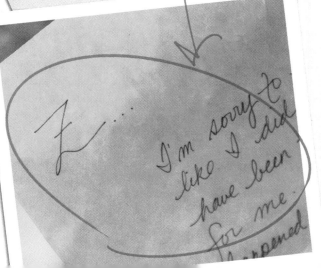

THE FACES OF HOLLYWOOD HIGH

Inga and Trish
My new friends—I think.

Inga's little brother, Corky

My to-do list:

- ☑ See janitor about checking out the traces of lead paint in utility shed.

- ☑ Talk to principal about a CPR course.

- ☐ Get healthier options in the cafeteria, such as a salad bar.

Corky may have a future in sleuthing. He's quite eager to solve this mystery with me!

$$x = \frac{-b \pm \sqrt{b^2 - 4ac}}{2a}$$

Tuesday evening

At school today I couldn't stop thinking about that letter I had found in the attic. So when I got home I decided to see if I could find anything else. This mansion is full of clues! There's an old projection room hidden in a hallway, and it's filled with Dehlia's films. While I was looking around, a man appeared behind me! It turned out to be the caretaker, Leshing. He seemed a bit creepy, so I decided to keep my eye on him.

Dehlia wrote a new will, and "Z" knew. Who is "Z"?

Name: ? Leshing

Occupation: Caretaker at the Draycott Mansion since 1971

Link to Dehlia: Worked at Dehlia's film studio after he got out of the military. Met Dehlia when he was sent to her mansion to project a movie for her. He stayed on as caretaker.

Notes: Cares deeply about Dehlia—enough to kill her? But why? Military background means he could be dangerous. Always lurking around the house. Lives in the apartment building down the hill from Draycott Mansion.

Wednesday
CLUE: The X

This afternoon I gathered all of the Dehlia things I have found. I saw a bunch of snapshots of Dehlia—on set and at movie premieres. I noticed that in the photos that were taken just before she disappeared she always seemed to be hiding her belly—or the photo only showed her from the shoulders up.

Did Dehlia get this robe at a hotel—or a hospital?

In one of the last photos of her ever taken, she was wearing a robe marked with an X.

Wednesday evening/Thursday morning

CLUE: The Secret Baby

This evening as I walked around the neighborhood, I spotted two palm trees that seemed strangely familiar. Together they made an X shape just like the one I had seen on Dehlia's robe! I did some research, and it turns out Dehlia had stayed at the Twin Palms resort right before her death—and the resort was close to a hospital. I wondered whether my hunch about her pregnancy was true, so I checked with the hospital. I was right! Dehlia had given birth to a daughter, Jane Brighton, before she died.

X marks the spot!

Thursday afternoon

After knocking on dozens of doors I finally found Jane Brighton today. Jane and her daughter, Allie, have had a difficult life and aren't exactly well-off, but they seem to be happy. I told Jane that she is Dehlia's daughter, and I promised to help her. If I can find that missing will, maybe then Jane and Allie won't have to worry about anything anymore.

Allie looks just like Dehlia Draycott, her grandmother!

Friday

CLUE: The Dream

Yesterday I met Dehlia's estate lawyer, Dashiel Biedermeyer. I tried to tell him about Jane, but he was very busy. Then last night I dreamed about Dehlia. She said, "The will is in the Chinese box." It seemed so real, as if she was actually trying to tell me something important. I know it's a long shot, but I'm going to check it out. I always like to follow my hunches.

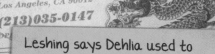
Leshing says Dehlia used to collect Chinese antiques, but some of them were sold off last year. He didn't remember the dealer's name, but I found this ad circled in the Yellow Pages.

Name: Dashiel Biedermeyer

Occupation: Famous Hollywood attorney

Link to Dehlia: Dehlia Draycott's estate lawyer

Notes:

- Always surrounded by several other lawyers.
- Obsessed with his status in Hollywood.
- Claims that all of his clients are movie stars.
- Connected to high-ranking government officials.

My roadster!

Name: Ned Nickerson

Occupation: Student; all-around good guy

Link to Dehlia: None!

Notes: Thank goodness, Ned brought the roadster! I couldn't solve this case without him or my car.

An early birthday surprise! Ned drove my car here all the way from River Heights!

Saturday afternoon
CLUE: The Antiques Store

Ned and my new friend Corky came with me to K. G. Louie today to search for the will. Inga and Trish joined us at the shop. Even with all five of us looking, we didn't find the will anywhere. Corky, Ned, and I returned to Draycott Mansion.

This black SUV keeps following us!

Saturday night
CLUE: The Tunnel

Tonight Ned, Corky, and I found a secret tunnel! It runs from the Draycott Mansion attic, through the mansion's walls, and all the way down the hill to an apartment building. That's the building where Leshing lives!

This must be how the intruder got into the mansion! Is Leshing the intruder?

Sunday, A Week Later

Tonight Jane came to the mansion. She was crying and very upset. "They took Allie," she said, "and I have nowhere else to go. I need your help!"

I did my best to calm her down so she could explain what had happened: Someone had threatened her, saying that if she ever tried to prove she was Dehlia's daughter, she would regret it. I promised to help her.

Monday afternoon
CLUE: The Movie

I finally figured out where my dream came from! It's one of Dehlia's movies. In the movie a priest shows Dehlia's character that she has to "make the dragon bow" on a box that I definitely saw in K. G. Louie's.

Monday night
CLUE: The Missing Will

I'm writing from my hospital bed—but first I have to record the rest of what happened today! I went back to K. G. Louie's and found the box. This time I made the dragon bow and easily opened the hidden compartment. I was reading the will in the parking lot when a familiar black SUV screeched up and a couple of men jumped out! They must have knocked me unconscious or something, because the next thing I knew I woke up in a dark room.

Monday night

The room was high above an old auditorium. Below me three men were watching one of Dehlia's old movies. The will was right beside them! So I quietly pulled out my sleuth kit and rigged up an instant will-retrieval device. But just as I held the will once again in my hands, the scaffolding I stood on came crashing down! While the men tried to figure out what had happened, I raced out of the building, found my car, and drove off as quickly as possible.

Last Will and Testament

of

DEHLIA DRAYCOTT

I, DEHLIA DRAYCOTT, of Los Angeles County, California, declare this to be my Will and revoke all other Wills.

ARTICLE I

I authorize my personal representative to pay such items as my personal representative deems proper for my cremation or burial and interment, including disposition of the ashes or acquisition of any burial site and the erection and of monuments and markers, regardless of any limitation fixed by statute court and without order of court.

ARTICLE II

Property and Assets

I thought I had escaped, but the black SUV appeared once more and slammed into my roadster. I spun out of control, crashing into a row of parked cars. So here I am in the hospital, recovering from just a few scratches and bruises. Good thing I was wearing my seat belt! When Dad came into my room, he looked so worried that I had to tell him everything. I couldn't lie to him! And I think he understands that I'm just trying to help Jane. Then Mr. Biedermeyer showed up. He had just been discussing some work with Dad.

(So much has happened since I left the hospital! Let's see if I can remember it all.)
Mr. Biedermeyer offered to drive us home. On the way there he said that he had been Dehlia's manager. This was news to me! I wondered if I should suspect him. Next thing I knew, he was signing a contract with a large "Z"—a "Z" I knew very well—and I rolled out of the speeding car, screaming at Dad to get out, too!

Biedermeyer's middle name is Zachary!

I wasn't far from Leshing's apartment building, so I raced up the path and knocked on the door. A woman answered and said I could use her phone. While I was on hold with the police, I asked her if she knew Biedermeyer. Guess what? He owns the entire apartment building—*and* Draycott Mansion!

By then I was sure Biedermeyer was "Z." He had gotten everything that had belonged to Dehlia because the will had been hidden since her death. I wasn't going to let him take what really belonged to Jane and Allie! As I saw the limo stop in front of the building, I sneaked into the tunnel in the basement and followed the dark passageway up to the mansion.

Suddenly a dark shape loomed out of the shadows. It was Mr. Biedermeyer! He grabbed my arms so I couldn't run. But he couldn't see that I had a voice recorder in one hand, and I had pressed RECORD.

Biedermeyer: "Where's that will?"
Me: "First tell me why you killed Dehlia."
Biedermeyer: "After she had the baby she was going to quit the business and run off with Leshing, the father. She was going to fire me—after all I had done for her! I got mad and reacted violently."

Now that I had recorded his confession, I slowly pulled the will out of my coat. Mr. Biedermeyer reached for it, but I was too quick for him. I dashed up the tunnel and clambered up the stairs.

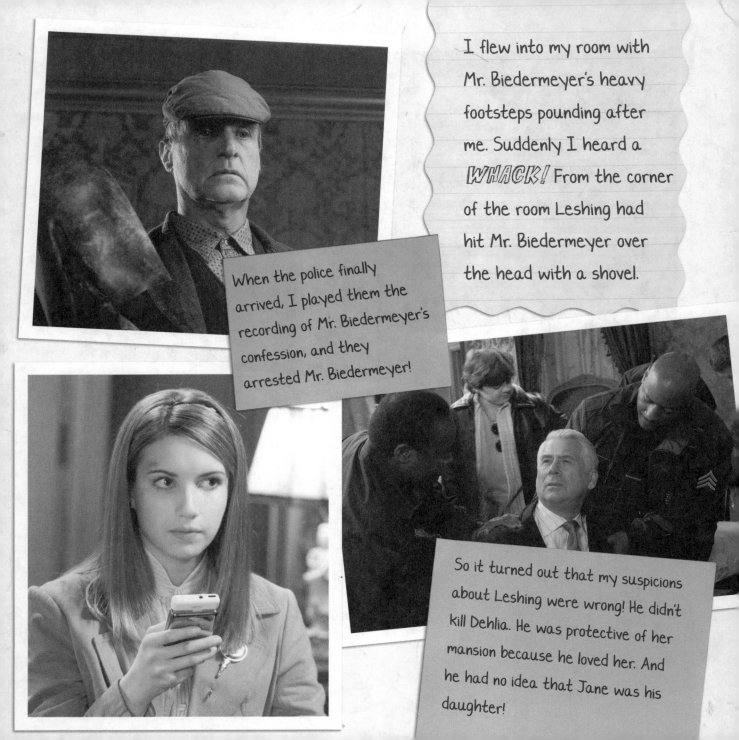

I flew into my room with Mr. Biedermeyer's heavy footsteps pounding after me. Suddenly I heard a **WHACK!** From the corner of the room Leshing had hit Mr. Biedermeyer over the head with a shovel.

When the police finally arrived, I played them the recording of Mr. Biedermeyer's confession, and they arrested Mr. Biedermeyer!

So it turned out that my suspicions about Leshing were wrong! He didn't kill Dehlia. He was protective of her mansion because he loved her. And he had no idea that Jane was his daughter!

Tuesday

What an exciting case! But the best part came later, when I was finally able to introduce Jane to her father, Leshing. It felt wonderful watching them meet for the first time after so many years. And, even better: This morning Dad found Allie and brought her home to Draycott Mansion! The mansion *is* Allie's new home, after all, since Dehlia actually left the mansion to Jane, not Mr. Biedermeyer.

A week later

Dad and I are about to get into the car with all of our stuff and make the long drive back to River Heights. I'll be glad to see my old friends back home, but I'm still sad to be leaving the ones I made here. Maybe someday I'll come back on another Hollywood case! But for now I'll take a break from seeking out more mysteries . . . unless they find me first!